Time and Again
Stories

Time and Again Stories

DONALD BISSET

METHUEN CHILDREN'S BOOKS

LONDON

For Amanda

A selection of these stories first appeared in
SOME TIME STORIES © *1957 by Donald Bisset*
THIS TIME STORIES © *1961 by Donald Bisset*
This volume first published 1970 by Methuen & Co. Ltd
Reprinted 1973
Second edition 1979
Methuen Children's Books Ltd
11 New Fetter Lane, London EC4P 4EE
Copyright © 1970 by Donald Bisset
Printed in Great Britain
by Richard Clay (The Chaucer Press) Ltd,
Bungay, Suffolk
ISBN 0 416 14490 X

Contents

The river of words

Once upon a time there was a river which was made of words. It flowed down to the sea and the sea was made of story books.

As the river flowed along, the words and the letters tumbled over each other and buffeted the rocks just like ordinary rivers.

"I know," said the river. "Let's write a story! Once upon a time. . . ."

"Hooray!" shouted all the other words. "That's the way to begin a story. Now what comes next?"

This is the story the river told them.

Once upon a time there was a river made of words and it was going down to the sea and all the words were going into story books, when suddenly a little otter swam across the river and the words got into the wrong order so that instead of writing "Once upon a time" it wrote "on a Once up time" and it got in a frightful muddle.

"Oh, you are a naughty otter," the river said to the otter whose name was Charlie. "Now you've spoilt our story."

"I'm terribly sorry!" said Charlie. "Perhaps if I swim back again it'll put things right."

He swam back and then clambered on the bank and looked at the words, "time upon a Once," he read. "Surely that's not right!"

However the river swirled about a bit and soon got it right. "Once upon a time," he read, "there was an otter whose name was Charlie."

"Why that's me! My name's Charlie. It's a story about me!" He got so excited and jumped up and down and then slipped and fell in the river and jumbled up the words again. Oh, the river was annoyed!

The otter got out as quickly as he could and looked at the words: "otter was Charlie time upon a Once". Worse and worse!

"What do you expect?" said the river. "Every time we

8

start you fall in and get it all jumbled. Now we've got to start all over again."

"Once upon a time there was an otter whose name was Charlie and he lived by the river of words. . . . Now what happens next?"

They thought and thought but couldn't think of a story about Charlie. So he said, "I'll help," and got back from the river and then ran as fast as he could and jumped right into the middle of the river. Then he swam ashore and looked at the words. (He'd jumbled them right, this time.)

"Once upon a time there was a very naughty otter," he read, "and one day he met a pussy cat."

"Mieow!" said the pussy cat. "Do you like ice-cream?"

"No!" said Charlie.

"Mieow! Do you like milk?"

"No!"

"Mieow! Do you like fish?"

"Yes, I do!" said Charlie.

"Mieow," said the pussy cat. "Well, if you come to my house my auntie will give you a fish tea. Brown bread and butter and fish paste."

"That will be nice!" said Charlie. "It makes me feel quite hungry. I think I'll go home to tea now. But before I go tell me, what are you going to do with the story?"

"It's going to be a story in a book called *Time and Again Stories*," said the river.

Charlie was pleased. "That's nice!" he said. "Now I'm going! Goodbye!"

"Goodbye!" said the river.

The words all jumbled around and then spelt "Love and kisses to Charlie". And tumbling and tossing they flowed on into the story-book sea.

The thin king
and the fat cook

Once upon a time there was a very fat King who said to his very thin cook, "Bake me a cake! The lightest, nicest, scrumpiest cake you've ever made."

So the cook got a big bowl and two dozen eggs and some butter and five pounds of flour and a pound of yeast.

He mixed the flour and the eggs and the butter in the big bowl, then put in the yeast. Then he lit the gas and when the oven was hot he put the cake in.

Soon there was a lovely smell of baking cake, and the King came running in.

"My, my!" he said. "What a lovely smell. I'm sure it's going to be a delicious cake, cook."

"Ah, yes, Your Majesty," said the cook, "and it's going to be the lightest cake in the world. I put in a whole pound of yeast to make it rise."

"That's the stuff!" said the King. "But what's this?" They looked round and saw that the top of the gas stove was beginning to bend and suddenly, with a *Crack*! it shot up in the air and the top of the cake appeared, rising slowly.

11

"Tch, tch!" said the King. "Now, look what you've done! You put in *too much* yeast!"

The cake went on rising until, at last, it was pressing against the ceiling, which began to crack.

The cook and the King rushed upstairs and when they got to the top they saw the cake had gone right through the ceiling to the floor above.

"Do something, my good man!" shouted the King. The poor cook didn't know what to do. So he jumped up and sat on the cake to stop it rising.

But it went on rising just the same till the cook felt his head bump on the ceiling. A moment later his head went through the roof and still the cake went on rising.

"Oh, Your Majesty! Please go and turn the gas off!" shouted the cook.

The King rushed downstairs and turned the gas off. Then he got his telescope and went into the garden.

The cake had stopped rising, but the top was very high up in the air.

"Oh, drat the man!" said the King. "If he doesn't come down soon there won't be anyone to cook the dinner." Then he thought, "If the cook was to start eating the cake, then he would get lower and lower." So he called out, "Cook, eat the cake, at once!"

"Delighted, Your Majesty," called back the cook, and he took a bite. "Yum, yum!" he said. "This *is* nice cake!"

"Oh, stop talking," said the King, "and eat it up as fast as you can, or I shall have no dinner."

"Right, Your Majesty," said the cook, and ate as fast as he could. But it was such a big cake that it took him two weeks to eat it all and it made him very fat. But the poor King who was waiting for his dinner, got thinner and thinner.

So instead of the King being fat and the cook being thin, there was a very thin King and a very fat cook!

"Never mind, Your Majesty," called the cook when he had eaten the cake and reached the ground. "I'll cook you a lovely dinner now!" And he did.

St Pancras and
King's Cross

Once upon a time there were two railway stations who lived right next door to each other. One was called St Pancras and the other King's Cross. They were always quarrelling as to which was the better station.

"I have diesel engines as well as steam engines at my station," said St Pancras.

"Humph! So have I!" said King's Cross.

"And I've got a cafeteria," said St Pancras.

"So have I!"

"Open on Sundays?"

"Yes, open on Sundays!"

"Humph!"

There was silence for a few minutes, then King's Cross said, "Well, I've got ten platforms and you've only got seven."

"I'm twice as tall as you are!" replied St Pancras. "And, anyway, your clock is slow."

The King's Cross clock was furious and ticked away as fast as it could to catch up. It ticked so fast that soon the St Pancras clock was away behind, and it ticked as fast as it could too, so as not to be out-done. They both got faster and faster; and the trains had to go faster too so as not to be late.

Quicker and quicker went the clocks and faster and faster went the trains, till at last they had no time even to set down their passengers, but started back again as soon as they had entered the station. The passengers were furious and waved their umbrellas out of the windows.

"Hi, stop!" they called. But the engines wouldn't.

"No!" they said. "We can't stop or we'll be late. Can't you see the time?"

By now the clocks were going so fast that almost as soon as it was morning it was evening again.

The sun was very surprised. "I must be going too slow!" it thought. So it hurried up and set almost as soon as it had risen and then rose again. The people all over London were in such a state getting up and going to bed, and then getting up again with hardly any sleep at all – and running to work so as not to be late, and the children running to school and hardly having time to say twice two are four and running home again.

Finally the Lord Mayor of London said to the Queen, "Your Majesty, this won't do! I think we ought to go and give a medal to Euston Station, then the other two will be so jealous they may stop quarrelling."

"That's a good idea!" said the Queen. So she set out from Buckingham Palace with the Lord Mayor and the Horse Guards and the Massed Bands of the Brigade of Guards, and in front of her walked the Prime Minister carrying a gold medal on a red velvet cushion.

When they got to King's Cross the two stations stopped quarrelling and looked at them.

"Do you see what I see, St Pancras?" asked King's Cross.

"I do indeed!" said St Pancras. "A medal being taken to Euston Station, just because it's got fifteen platforms. It's not fair! Why, you're a better station than Euston!"

"And so are you, St Pancras," said King's Cross.

St Pancras was surprised, but it thought it would be nice to be friends after all the quarrelling, so it said, "Let's be friends."

"Yes, let's!" said King's Cross.

So they became friends and stopped quarrelling, and their clocks stopped going too fast and their trains stopped having to hurry. Everyone was very pleased.

"You are clever, Lord Mayor!" said the Queen.

"Thank-you, Your Majesty," said the Lord Mayor.

The hot potato

Once upon a time there lived a cow whose name was Dot, who was very fond of hot potatoes. One day she swallowed one whole without chewing it, and it was so hot inside her that it hurt, and she began to cry. Great big tears rolled down her cheeks.

The farmer, whose name was Mr Smith, got a bucket to catch the tears in, so that they wouldn't make the floor all wet.

"Whatever is the matter Dot?" he said.

"I swallowed a hot potato," said Dot.

"You poor thing," said Mr Smith, "open your mouth."

Dot opened her mouth and smoke came out. What was to be done? Mr Smith picked up the bucket of tears and poured it down Dot's throat. There was a sort of sizzling noise, and Dot smiled because she felt better.

That evening, when Dot was lying in her byre, eating some hay, she made up a song:

> *When you eat potatoes hot,*
> *Be sure you chew them quite a lot*
> *Or you'll get a pain inside,*
> *Like the time I did and cried,*
> *Because I didn't stop to chew*
> *My potato through and through.*
> *What a silly cow I am!*
> *What a silly cow I am!*

19

Dot stopped and she sharpened her pencil. "Now, what rhymes with 'am'?" she thought.

> *Jam and spam and pram and tram,*
> *I'll send myself a telegram:*
> *'This is to remind you, not*
> *To eat potatoes when they're hot.'*
> *Address the telegram to cow.*

And that is all Dot wrote because, just then, she fell asleep.

The winding road

Once upon a time a little blue car was going along a winding road.

"Why are you so bendy?" it said to the road.

"Well," said the road, "shall I tell you the story of how I was made?"

"Yes, please!" said the little blue car. "Tell me the story."

"Well," said the road, "some men with pick-axes and shovels made me. I started off straight, and, after a little while, I met a cow who was lying asleep so I said, 'Wake up, Cow! I'm the new road just being made. I want to go straight and you are in the way.'

"The cow opened her eyes and said, 'Moo!' But she wouldn't go away, even though the men went and shouted in her ear. So they built the road (that's me) round her; and that was the first bend.

"Then, when they had gone a little farther, a bull in the field bellowed at the men very fiercely so they turned away, and that was the second bend.

"After that one of the men said, 'I would like a nice ice-cream!'

" 'So would I!' said the others.

"So they bent me round to the place where the ice-cream shop was and they each bought an ice-cream, and that was the third bend. Then they all lay down to sleep.

"When they woke up the foreman said, 'Now, lads! Let's be getting on with it!' So they got up and started again, but they were still so sleepy they didn't notice where they were going and went the wrong way around another bend. That was the fourth!

" 'Hi!' said the big foreman. 'You're going the wrong way. We're supposed to go that way!' And he pointed a different way. So they turned a fifth bend and went that way.

"After a while they saw a hen who had a family of chickens.

" 'Will you please move your chicks?' said the men. 'They are in the way.'

" 'Well, there's one more egg to hatch yet,' said the hen.

" 'Oh, no!' said the men. 'That will take too long!' So they built me round them.

"By then it was nearly time to go home, so they put their pick-axes and shovels away and the foreman looked at me. 'You're not very straight, are you?' he said. 'Oh well, never mind!' And then he went home.

"So you see, little blue car, that's why I am so bendy," said the road.

"I do see!" said the little blue car. "I do like bendy roads. Toot-toot!"

The tiger who liked baths

Once upon a time there was a tiger whose name was Bert. He had big, white, sharp teeth and when he growled it made a noise like thunder.

But Bert was a very nice tiger, always kind and gentle, except when someone else wanted to have a bath.

He loved having a bath and lay in the water all day until Mr and Mrs Smith and their baby daughter, who lived with him, were very cross. Because every time they wanted to have a bath Bert growled and showed his teeth.

"Come on, Bert! Do come out and have your supper," said Mrs Smith, holding out a big plate of bones.

"No, thank you," said Bert, and growled.

Poor Mrs Smith nearly cried. "It's time to bath the baby," she said, "and there's Bert still in the bath. Whatever shall I do?"

"I know what we'll do," said Mr Smith, and he went and bought twenty bottles of black ink and, when Bert wasn't looking, he poured them into his bath. It made the water all black so that Bert got all black too.

A few hours later Bert decided it was supper time so he got out of the bath.

"Oh, look at that big black pussy cat," said Mr Smith.

"Oh, yes, what a beautiful pussy cat!" said Mrs Smith.

"Pussy cat?" said Bert. "I'm not a pussy cat. I'm a tiger."

"Tigers have stripes," said Mr Smith. "They are not black all over like you."

"Oh dear!" said Bert, "perhaps I am a pussy cat, after all."

"And pussy cats," said Mr Smith, "don't like having baths. You know that!"

"That's true!" said Bert.

After supper Bert went into the garden. And Prince, the dog next door, who liked chasing pussy cats, saw Bert, and said, "There's a pussy cat! I'll chase him!"

He felt a bit nervous because Bert looked the biggest pussy cat he had ever seen. Still, pussy cats had always run away before when he barked at them so he ran up to Bert, barking and showing his teeth.

25

Bert turned his head lazily and growled just once, like this: GRRRRRRRRRRRRR!

Prince had never been so frightened in his life, and he jumped over the fence and ran home.

A little later, when Mr Smith came into the garden, Bert asked him, "Am I really a pussy cat? Don't you think I'm too big?"

"Well, you're not *really* a pussy cat," said Mr Smith. "You're a tiger. A special kind of tiger, who never likes staying in the bath for more than half an hour. And that's the very best kind of tiger."

Bert *was* pleased. "That kind!" he said to himself. "The very best kind!" And he purred and then licked all the black off till he was a lovely yellow tiger again with black stripes.

Then he went into the house and said to Mr Smith, "I think I'll just go and have a bath." And he turned the water on and had a lovely bath. But he stayed in the water only for half an hour, and Mrs Smith said he was a very good tiger and gave him a big bucket of ice-cream.

Bert put his head in the bucket and licked. "Yum! yum! yum!" he said. "I do like ice-cream."

Nelson's egg

One warm summer day, Lord Nelson was standing on top of his tall column when a little cloud came sailing by.

"Please wash my face," said Lord Nelson.

"Certainly," said the cloud, and it rained on Lord Nelson till his face was clean.

"Thank-you," said Nelson, "I suppose you are a magic cloud, aren't you?"

"Well, my lord, I suppose I am," said the cloud.

"Of course you are," said Lord Nelson, "Only magic clouds can talk and that proves it. But, you know, little cloud, I get rather lonely up here, just being a statue, with no one to talk to."

"You just look through your telescope," said the cloud, "and if you see someone you'd like to talk to I'll go and tell them."

So Lord Nelson put his telescope to his good eye and looked all round Trafalgar Square and up the Strand and down Whitehall and along St Martin's Lane and there, in St Martin's Lane, he saw a chicken crossing the road.

"Why does a chicken cross the road?" said Lord Nelson to the cloud.

"I don't know," said the little cloud. "Shall I fetch her?"

"Yes, please!" said Lord Nelson.

So the little cloud went and said to the chicken, "Lord Nelson would like to talk to you."

The chicken was very pleased and went over to Nelson's Column and Lord Nelson let down a piece of string and the chicken climbed and climbed and climbed until she got to the top. Nelson was pleased to see her.

"What is your name?" he said.

"Martha, my lord," said the chicken.

"Now why," said Lord Nelson, "why does a chicken cross the road?"

"Well, my lord," said Martha, "when I lay an egg on one side of the road so that someone on that side can have an egg for breakfast, to lay the next egg, I cross the road so that someone on the other side can have an egg for breakfast too."

"An egg for breakfast!" said Lord Nelson, dreamily. He gave a big sigh and a tear rolled down his cheek.

"Don't cry, my lord," said Martha, "I'll stay with you and lay you an egg for breakfast every morning."

And so she did.

Sometimes the little cloud passes and rains so that they can wash their faces, and sometimes they have a little talk. Lord Nelson isn't lonely any longer and he always has an egg for breakfast.

The grasshopper and
the snail

Once upon a time there was a grasshopper who was very very proud and his name was Sandy. When he was a baby grasshopper and learning to hop with the other baby grasshoppers, he always hopped great big hops, and the teacher said, "You must hop little hops as well as big ones, Sandy."

"No," said Sandy, "I'm an important grasshopper. I'm only going to hop *big* hops." So he never learned to hop little hops at all.

Well, one day, when he was out for a hop, he met a snail whose name was Olive.

"Don't you find things rather slow, my dear?" he said to her. "Crawling along all day with your house on your back?"

"Oh no," said Olive. "I like crawling. And I like being a snail, especially when it rains, because I never get wet under my nice shell. And I'm never late home because I'm here all the time, if you see what I mean. So it's fun being a snail."

"Oh, well," said Sandy, "there's no accounting for tastes I suppose. Good-bye!" And he hopped away. He *was* proud! Still, he was very good at hopping. Grasshoppers are. Sandy could hop twelve inches at one hop

which is a lot of hop when you are only an inch long. But there was one thing Sandy couldn't do, of course. He couldn't hop small hops. He couldn't hop say six inches or three inches but only twelve inches. Every time – twelve inches.

After he had finished talking to Olive Snail it was teatime so he started to hop home. But when he was nearly there – just six inches from his house, which was a little hole – he found he couldn't get in because every time he hopped, he hopped right over his house and found himself on the other side. He tried again and again but because he could only hop big hops, he always hopped over his hole and never into it.

Poor Sandy was getting very tired and ever so cross when

who should come crawling by but Olive, with her house on her back.

"There, you see, Sandy," she said, "it has its advantages being a snail. At least one can get home without any bother."

However she was a kind snail. (Most snails are, except when they wake up first thing in the morning – then they are a bit grouchy.) So she said to Sandy, "If you get on my back I'll give you a ride."

So Sandy got on her back and she crawled home with him. He *was* pleased! "Thank-you, dear Olive," he said. "I see now that hopping *big* hops isn't everything."

"That's true!" said Olive. "Little hops are just as nice as big ones. Bye bye, Sandy."

Olive Snail
and Geldie

Thousands of years ago, when the King of Tipperary was a very young man, a canary sang in a golden cage at the bottom of the King's garden. The canary's name was Geldie.

One morning when he was having his breakfast – he had cornflakes with milk and sugar – he ate so fast that he swallowed some down the wrong way and nearly choked. He coughed and coughed and coughed.

He coughed so loudly that a snail, whose name was Olive, who lived at the other end of the King's garden, got very worried and decided to hurry across the garden to pat Geldie on the back so that he could stop coughing and finish his breakfast.

First of all Olive Snail sent a letter to her mother to say where she was going.

Mrs. G. Snail,
The Potato Patch,
Bottom of the Garden,
The Palace,
Tipperary.

Then she started off. All day long the hot sun beat down on her, but she struggled bravely on, determined to help him, and at dusk she arrived at Geldie's cage.

Poor Geldie was still coughing, so Olive patted him on the back as hard as she could with her horns. What a relief it was, because you see, the patting loosed the corn-flakes and Geldie stopped coughing, and felt so pleased that he opened his beak and sang.

Olive was charmed, she felt she could listen to him for hours, and wished that she could sing too. After that, they became great friends and went to tea with each other nearly every day.

Ring! Ring!

Once upon a time there was a man and a telephone. The telephone went, "Ring ring! Ring ring! Ring!"

"Hello!" said the man, picking up the receiver.

His wife, who was far away, spoke.

36

"Hello!" she said, "I can't find the cat's dinner. Where did you put it? The poor little thing is ever so hungry!"

"What a shame!" said the man. "I put the cat's dinner in the refrigerator."

All the words he said rushed along the telephone line back to his wife, at the other end of the wire. All except the last word, REFRIGERATOR, which was such a big word – bigger than all the others – that it got very squashed in the wire. It couldn't go as fast as the little words, so it got left behind and began to cry.

"I'll go back the other way again," it decided. What a fuss there was! It had to squeeze past other words.

"Oh, don't push!" they said. "You're going the wrong way."

The man was very surprised when the word came back. "You are silly!" he said. "I told my wife to look in the refrigerator for the cat's dinner. If she didn't hear me say 'REFRIGERATOR', she won't know where to look and the cat won't get any dinner. It will get thinner and thinner till there is nothing left of it but its mieow. You wouldn't like that to happen, would you?

"Now, you be a good word and I'll send you off again and mind you don't get stuck this time," the man added. So he listened very carefully.

"Where did you say the cat's dinner was?" he heard his wife ask.

"I said it's in the refrigerator," he said.

This time the REFRIGERATOR word was ready to have

37

a really good try. Off it went along the wire, faster than a space rocket. In fact it went so fast it almost reached the end before all the other words in the sentence, and that wouldn't have been very helpful. So it got to the other end at the right time – exactly right.

The lady was very pleased indeed and sent it back. "All right! I'll look in the refrigerator," she said.

So the cat got its dinner.

Fog

Once upon a time, on the Queen's birthday, the fog had come to London to see the Trooping of the Colour. But when it got there the Queen said to the General, "We won't have Trooping the Colour today because it's foggy."

And this happened every time the fog came. So it felt sad, it did want to see Trooping the Colour. But how could it if every time it came to London the Queen said, "Cancel the Parade"?

Now, at Buckingham Palace, under the Queen's chair, there lived a cat, whose name was Smokey, and he felt very sorry for the fog and wanted to help it. So next year, just before the Queen's birthday, he wrote it a letter:

UNDER THE QUEEN'S CHAIR
THE PALACE.

TUESDAY.
DEAR FOG,
PLEASE COME TO
THE PALACE.
YOURS SINCERELY,
SMOKEY.

That night, before she went to bed the Queen put the cat out at the back door at Buckingham Palace and went up-stairs to bed. And, sure enough, before Smokey had time to mieow three times, he saw the fog. They were pleased to see each other.

"I do want to see Trooping the Colour," said the fog. "But they always cancel the parade when it's foggy so I never get to see it."

"I know," said Smokey. "Now, tomorrow you must arrive just as the soldiers are going on parade and when the General sees you he'll say, 'Your Majesty, there's a fog. Shall I cancel the parade?' "

"Yes, he always says that," said the fog with a sigh.

"Then," continued Smokey, "just as the Queen is going to say, 'Yes, cancel the parade!' you mieow."

"All right!" said the fog. "But how do I mieow?"

So Smokey showed him and the fog practised till it was good at mieowing.

Next morning the soldiers were all lined up for the parade when the General said, "Shall I cancel the parade, Your Majesty? I see a fog."

"Where?" said the Queen.

"There!" said the General, pointing to the fog.

Just then the fog mieowed.

"Really, General," said the Queen. "Can't you tell the fog from a pussy cat? I distinctly heard it mieow. Of course you can't cancel the parade!"

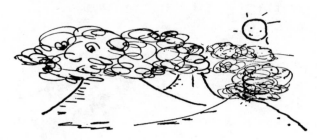

So the fog stayed and saw Trooping the Colour after all. It felt happy now and went away to live on top of the mountains in Wales where there were other fogs to play with.

Once the Queen wrote to it:

The Palace.
1st. June.

Dear Fog,
Please stay away,
Yours sincerely,
The Queen.

And the fog wrote back:

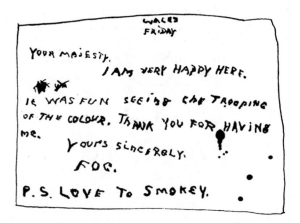

The Queen can't understand it. "How did the fog manage to see Trooping the Colour, Smokey?" she asks him, looking under her chair.

But Smokey just purrs. That's his secret.

Annabelle

Once upon a time there was a cow with a poorly tummy. Her name was Annabelle. And one day she saved a big ship from being wrecked.

One foggy day, on the coast of Cornwall, Annabelle was in her field eating some grass for breakfast. The fog was so thick that she couldn't see the end of her nose, and suddenly she swallowed a thistle.

Oh dear! It was in her tummy and prickled and hurt like anything. Annabelle stopped eating and mooed as loudly as she could.

Just then a big ship was sailing by on her way to America.

The Captain looked through his telescope but he could see only fog.

"Do you know where we are?" he said to his first officer.

"No, Sir! But we're somewhere off the coast of Cornwall."

"Well, sound the hooter," said the Captain. So the first officer sounded the hooter – 'Moooo!'

Annabelle heard it, and thought, "There's another cow who has swallowed a thistle. I must get the doctor," and she mooed to let the other cow know she had heard.

"Listen!" said the Captain. The first officer stopped sounding the hooter and listened. Then, from across the water, through the fog, they heard it again: "Moo!"

"That's Annabelle Cow," said the Captain. "We must be near her field." And he started giving lots of orders.

"Stip the shop! I mean – Stop the ship!"

"Reverse the engines!"

"Drop the anchor!"

"Sound the hooter!"

The ship stopped, the anchor chain rattled down and the ship's siren sounded again: 'Moooo!'

"Oh, what a poorly tummy that cow's got," thought Annabelle, and she mooed again, "Moooo!"

The Captain looked over the side. Soon the sun came out and the Captain saw that he had stopped the ship from hitting a big rock.

He had saved his ship, all because he had heard Annabelle's moos.

Just then, he heard her mooing again, "Mooooo! Mooooo!"

"That's funny," he thought, "She's still mooing, perhaps she's got a poorly tummy!" So he sent the ship's doctor ashore to make Annabelle's tummy better.

"And give her this too!" he said, and handed the doctor a little box with a big label tied to it.

When the doctor reached the shore, Annabelle was still feeling poorly, but he gave her some pills and she soon began to feel all right.

"The Captain asked me to give you this," said the doctor. He took the little box the Captain had given him and showed it to her. On the label was written:

'To Annabelle – The Cow that saved our Ship – From the Captain.'

Inside was a lovely silver medal. The doctor tied it round Annabelle's neck and the medal hung on her chest. She *was* proud.

"That's because by mooing you saved the ship. Now I must hurry back because we are going to America," said the doctor.

He hurried to the ship. The sun shone brightly and the fog had gone.

Annabelle looked out to sea.

"Moo!" she said.

'Moo!' replied the ship.

As the ship sailed on, the moos became fainter. But the Captain, looking through his telescope, could see Annabelle eating grass with the medal round her neck.

"Moo!" said Annabelle, looking out to sea. "Moo!"

And from the big ship, far across the water, she thought she heard a faint 'Moo!'

She was very happy and went on eating her grass, while the medal shone in the morning sunlight.

The horse and the apple tree

Once upon a time there was a little apple tree that was just growing up. One day a horse came along and decided that he'd wait there till some apples had grown and then have a good meal.

"I'll eat your apples for you!" said the horse to the tree. The tree felt glad at first, then it began to be worried.

"I'm not quite sure how to grow apples!" it thought. So it asked a thistle that was growing nearby, and the thistle told the tree how it thought apples should be grown.

The tree took the thistle's advice and, in the autumn, it grew not apples – but thistles.

It was very upset. And so was the thistle, who had meant well. The horse was even more upset. "I'll have to wait till next year, now, for apples!" he thought.

Well, the next year the tree was determined to grow apples properly and one day, when a squirrel was scampering along its branches, it asked the squirrel how *he* thought apples should be grown. The squirrel told it and it took the squirrel's advice and, that year, it grew not apples – but squirrels, who wriggled till they dropped on to the ground and scampered away.

The tree and the horse were both upset. So one day, when the farmer, whose tree it was, came along with his wife, the tree swished its leaves in the wind. The farmer pointed to it and said, "This little apple tree grew thistles in its first year, squirrels in the second year. I wonder what it will grow this year?"

"Fancy, a squirrel tree!" said his wife. "Perhaps it doesn't know how to grow apples."

"Hm! That's true!" said the farmer, and went on to say how *he* thought apples should be grown. And his wife agreed with him.

The tree listened very carefully and took their advice, and next year, grew not apples – but babies.

The farmer's wife was pleased. She was very fond of babies. "They're so nice to cuddle!" she said. "And they smell all milky."

But, presently, they began to cry. What a noise they made!

After that the horse became very thoughtful. "I wonder," he said out loud, glancing at the tree, "I wonder what's the best way to grow horses?"

The tree thought for a bit then it told the horse how *it* would grow horses. The horse listened very carefully and remembered everything the apple tree said. And one day, soon after, when the tree asked, "Dear horse, please tell me, how would *you* grow apples?" The horse looked at the tree and told it word for word exactly what *it* had said about how to grow horses.

"I'll take your advice!" said the tree and for the first time, felt rather more sure of itself.

"Aha! you're taking your own advice!" thought the horse, "and that's how it should be!"

The horse was quite right, for the very next autumn, the tree bore loads of lovely red apples.

"Ah!" said the horse. "I do like apples!"

The puddle and the bun

Once upon a time there was a little puddle on the pavement. It had been raining and the water was still dripping from the glistening leaves on the trees. People walked by and a passing bus was reflected red in the water.

"Well, this is life," thought the puddle. "It's better than living in a cloud. All the same, I wish someone would drink me. After all, that's what water's for!"

53

Just then a great big van full of currant buns came along and, as it passed, one fell off with a splash right in to the puddle.

"Dear, oh dear me," said the bun. "Now I'm all wet and no one will eat me. I do feel sad!" And it began to cry.

"Oh, please don't cry," said the puddle. "Please don't cry."

"You're very kind," said the bun. "But, you see, though it's nice here with all the people passing and the red buses, and the trees dripping water, it's not so nice for a bun as being eaten, and I was on my way to the cafeteria at the station. I was going to be sold as a station bun and eaten with a cup of tea. Oh dear. Oh dear."

54

"Now don't cry," said the puddle. "Don't cry, dear bun!"

"I won't!" replied the bun. "I'm glad to have met you. Wouldn't it be fun if someone would come along and eat me and drink you?"

"Oh, yes," said the puddle. "But look. . . . Can you see what I see?"

There, coming towards them, was a mother duck and three little ducklings. A policeman put up his hand to stop the cars and buses while they crossed the road.

"And where are you going?" asked the policeman.

"Quack!" said the mother duck. "We're going to the pond." And all the little baby ducks said, "Squeek squeek squeek!" and followed their mother across the road.

"Oh, I do feel tired!" thought the mother duck. "And all the children should have a rest and something to eat." Then she saw the currant bun and the puddle. "Quack quack quack!" she said. "Look, there's a lovely currant bun and a puddle!" They were pleased!

"Goodbye, dear puddle," said the bun.

"Goodbye, my dear," replied the water.

"Yum yum yum," said the little ducks. "We do like buns and puddle water."

The buses passed, people walked by, and as the sun went down, the rain dripped from the trees and made a new puddle on the pavement, and the stars, coming out one by one in the sky overhead were reflected in the water.

"Honk honk honk," said the buses.

"Quack quack quack," said the baby ducks.

"Drip – drip – drip," went the rain.

And that is the end of the story.

The Emperor's mouse

Once upon a time, long, long ago, there lived an Emperor. This Emperor had a little mouse whose name was Misha.

Misha lived in the Emperor's pocket, and sometimes he came out and ran about the room and up the Emperor's sleeve.

One day, when the Emperor was sitting on his throne telling people what to do, a messenger arrived and bowed very low and said, "Your Majesty! Your mother is coming to tea and she is bringing her cat, Suki, with her."

"Oh, dear!" said the Emperor. "Suki is the best mouser in the whole of the empire. She'll be sure to catch Misha. Whatever shall we do?"

Just then some trumpeters outside blew their trumpets.

"It's your mother," said the messenger. "She is here already!"

"Quick!" said the Emperor, "pass me that thick envelope."

He got some scissors and cut some holes in it. Then he took a pen and addressed the envelope to himself. At the bottom in big letters he wrote: WITH CARE – DO NOT DROP.

Then, just as his mother and Suki were coming up the path, the Emperor stuck a stamp on the envelope. He put a little bit of cheese inside it. Then he took Misha out of his pocket and put him in the envelope and stuck it down.

"Now hurry out the back way," he said to the messenger, "and post this."

Then the Emperor kissed his mother and said, "Would you like some tea?"

58

"Yes, please!" she said. So he gave her some.

Meanwhile Suki was prowling around sniffing everywhere, to see if she could find a mouse to catch. But she couldn't.

Next day, after his mother and Suki had gone home, the postman came to the palace with a letter for the Emperor.

"It's a very wriggly letter, Your Majesty!" said the postman.

The Emperor took it and smiled. "I *wonder* what's in it?" he said. He opened it – and there was Misha inside, quite safe.

"I *am* glad to see you, Misha," said the Emperor, holding the mouse in his hand. And then he put him in his pocket.

Upside-down land

Once upon a time there was a crow whose name was Albert. Albert was a very lazy crow. Sometimes he fell asleep even when he was flying, and dreamed all sorts of strange things.

One day he fell sound asleep and, flying upside-down, he dreamed an upside-down dream. And this is it:

A cat, whose name was Marmy, liked chasing mice. He had found two mice in the laundry basket. He was just going to chase them when he heard one of the mice say, "Look, there's a pussy cat. Let's have fun and chase it."

Marmy *was* surprised. "That's all wrong. Mice don't chase cats!" he thought. But the mice *did* chase him and Marmy was so surprised that he ran away as fast as he could.

"This is an upside-down world!" he thought. Just then Butch came along. Butch was a big dog and he growled at Marmy.

Marmy was just going to run away and climb a tree when he thought, "Well, if it really *is* an upside-down world perhaps the dog will run away if I chase him."

So Marmy ran towards Butch as fast as he could. And, sure enough, Butch ran away.

"Well, this is a funny world!" thought Marmy. "Cats chase dogs, and mice chase cats. Well, I've never heard of such a thing before!"

He looked up. Coming down the road was a milkman and his horse and cart.

To Marmy's surprise the milkman was pulling the cart and the horse was sitting in the driving seat saying "Gee up!" to the milkman who started running down the road.

Then he saw two very small children coming along with their mother and father, and the children were saying to their parents, "You are very naughty. You must go to bed as soon as you get home and we won't give you any supper."

"Boo-hoo. Please don't punish us," said the mother and father.

It began to grow dark and instead of the moon and stars shining the sun rose.

"But it's night-time now," said Marmy. "The moon and stars should shine at night, not the sun. Go away, sun!"

"No," said the sun. "It's an upside-down world and I'm going to shine at night. Then I can play all day."

"Whatever next," thought Marmy. Then, looking up, he saw Albert, the crow, flying upside-down. "Why, Albert is sound asleep," he said. "He must be having an upside-down dream. Hey! Wake up, Albert!"

Albert woke up with a start, twirled round and flew the right way up. In the twinkling of an eye the sun went down. The moon rose and the stars came out. The milkman's horse pulled the milk cart, and Butch chased Marmy. Marmy chased the mice all the way back to the laundry basket. Then he was hungry so he went to the kitchen and had some nice fish and milk.

Albert flew back to his nest in the tree-tops to settle down to a long sleep.

"Caw!" he said. "That *was* a funny dream."

Rice pudding

Once upon a time there was a sad rice pudding. There it was in the cuboard next to the cheese.

"What shall I do?" it said. "Mary and John didn't like me at dinner!" and it began to cry.

"Never mind!" said the cheese. "If I were you, I'd ask the children's dreams to help me."

"The children's dreams?" said the rice pudding, who had never heard of dreams before. "Who are they?"

"Oh, I forgot. You wouldn't know about dreams," said the cheese. "You were only made today, but I've been here for a week, and I've often seen them."

"Where do they live?" asked the rice pudding.

"I'm not quite sure," said the cheese, "but every night, after the children's mother has tucked them up in bed, their dreams come in through the window and snuggle down beside them. Mary's dream usually comes first because she falls asleep quicker than John. But, as soon as he's asleep, John's dream comes too."

"I'd like to meet them," said the rice pudding. "Will they come tonight, do you think? If they do, I'll ask them to make the children like me."

64

"I should, if I were you," said the cheese. "They'll be here quite soon now."

That night, at bedtime, the rice pudding called out through the keyhole to Marmy, the cat, "Would you please ask John's and Mary's dreams to come and talk to me before they get into the children's beds tonight?"

"All right!" said Marmy. He was very fond of rice pudding. So he jumped on to the bedroom window-sill, and waited.

When the children were asleep, their dreams arrived and were just going inside the room when Marmy said, "Would you please go and talk to the rice pudding in the cupboard? It's ever so unhappy because the children don't like it."

"Don't like their rice pudding?" said the dreams. "All right!" And they went to the kitchen cupboard.

The rice pudding was pleased to see them. "Thank-you for coming!" it said. "When the children are asleep, will you whisper in their ears how nice rice pudding really is?"

"Of course!" said the dreams. "Of course we will. Now don't you worry, you'll soon be eaten up."

The rice pudding was very relieved. "Goodbye," it said, "and thank-you very much."

Back in the bedroom the dreams crept into the children's beds and told them how delicious to eat rice pudding really was, and how some was down in the cupboard with the cheese and the butter and wanted to be liked. Rice puddings always do!

Presently the dreams fell asleep too. But in the morning they woke first and, as the children woke up, the dreams floated out of the bedroom window.

It was a lovely day. The children played in the garden all morning and were very hungry by dinner time. After they had eaten most of their dinner, Mother said, "Would you like some rice pudding now?"

"Yes please!" said John.

"Ooh, yes Mummy!" said Mary.

Mummy was rather surprised. She had expected the children to say they didn't want rice pudding. Of course she didn't know anything about the dreams. But the children remembered them. Mummy gave each a great big helping and had some herself.

"It *is* good, isn't it, John?" said Mary as she tried a spoonful.

"Yes, just as I dreamed it would be," said John.

"Did you dream about the rice pudding too?" said Mary. "How odd!"

The rice pudding didn't say a word that anyone could hear, but to itself it said, "I do like being liked!"

The quacking pillarbox

Once upon a time there was a pillarbox. He was very beautiful and held the letters safely inside him till the postman came to collect them.

Very close to the pillarbox there stood a lamp. They were great friends. The lamp shone in the dark so that

people could see their way home, and could see to post their letters.

One night the lamp said to the pillarbox, "I believe I've caught a cold, I'm going to sneeze."

And he sneezed so hard his light went out. Now nobody could see to post their letters. What were they to do?

Just then a duck was walking by. Her name was Miranda. She thought, "Dear me! The lamp has gone out; how will people know where the pillarbox is, so as to post their letters?"

She climbed on top of the pillarbox and started quacking. She quacked and quacked and quacked, and all the people who were coming to post their letters, and couldn't find the pillarbox because the lamp was out, thought, "Whatever is all that quacking for?"

They went to where the noise was and saw Miranda quacking, and there, underneath Miranda, was the pillarbox. So they posted their letters in him and went home.

Under the carpet

Once upon a time there was a tiger and a horse who were great friends and they lived under the carpet in the drawing-room.

They liked living in the drawing-room because they liked drawing.

Sheila, the little girl who lived in the house, once asked them, "How do you get flat so as to get under the carpet?"

"Because we're imaginary animals," they said.

"I'm an imaginary tiger."

"And I'm an imaginary horse."

"And where do you keep your hay?" Sheila asked the horse.

"Under the carpet," he said. "It's imaginary hay."

"And do you keep your bones there, too?" she asked the tiger.

"Yes!" he said. "Bones!" And, licking his lips, he disappeared under the carpet. The horse followed him and Sheila was left alone.

Then she got some paper and drew pictures of lumps of sugar on it and put the piece of paper under the carpet. Presently she heard a crunching sound and a pleased sort of horsy voice saying, "Yum, yum, yum."

Then she wrote on a small piece of paper, "What do tigers like?" and put it under the carpet. There was a whispering noise then the horse poked his head out.

"Hay sandwiches," he said.

Sheila looked at him. "You're a naughty horse! Hay sandwiches are what horses like, aren't they? Now go and ask the tiger what he would like."

The horse went and the tiger came out. "I'd like a wristwatch," he said. "So that I can tell the time."

"All right!" said Sheila, and she drew the wristwatch and gave it to him; and some hay sandwiches for the horse. He disappeared. Presently they both came out.

"Thank-you very much, Sheila!" they said, and gave her a kiss.

"Is there anything else you'd like tonight?" she asked them. "It's nearly my bedtime."

"There is one thing we'd like," they said. "An umbrella."

"An umbrella!" said Sheila. "But it doesn't rain under the carpet. Oh, I forgot! It's imaginary rain!"

"Of course!" they said.

So she drew them an umbrella and gave it to them.

70

"Thank you!" they said. "Good night!"

"Good night!" said Sheila, and went up to bed. Then she thought, "Wouldn't it be dreadful to have a lovely new umbrella and then for it not to rain!" So she drew some rain on a big piece of paper and tip-toed downstairs and slipped it under the carpet.

Next morning when she came down, the drawing-room was a foot deep in water and the tiger and the horse were sitting in the umbrella which was opened and floating upside-down like a boat.

"I must have drawn too much rain!" thought Sheila.

After breakfast, when she came back to the drawing-room, Mummy was sweeping the carpet. There was no water and no umbrella and no tiger and no horse.

She sat down with her drawing-book and began to draw a tiger and a horse both sound asleep. Presently Mummy went out. Sheila sat and stared into the fire and all was quiet in the drawing-room except for the sound of snoring from under the carpet.

Bath night

Once upon a time there lived a beautiful black beetle whose name was Joe. He lived with his mother and father and fourteen sisters and eleven brothers in a crack in the wall of a big house.

He was the eldest beetle, and used to help his mother on bath nights by washing and scrubbing and drying and polishing his brothers and sisters. Then, when they were all tucked up in bed, he used to go for a walk in the garden and smell the flowers and have a talk with the other beetles or caterpillars or any friendly creature.

But one day, as he was walking across the grass, it started to pour with rain and Joe got very wet. So he thought, "I'll just go and sit in front of the fire in the sitting-room in the big house and get dry before I go home."

He crawled in, and there in front of the fire, he saw all the letters of the alphabet drying themselves. It had been their bath night too.

There was big A with a towel, drying all the little letters who had come down from the bath-room where big G had given them a bath. When they saw Joe they all crowded round him.

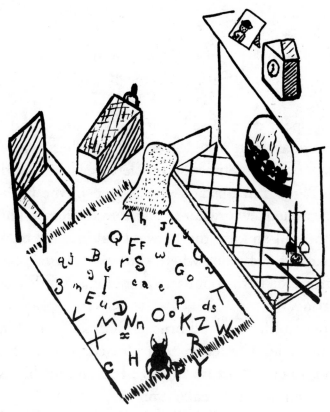

"What's your name?" they asked.

"Joe," said Joe.

"Shall we spell it for you?"

"Yes, please!" said Joe who had never yet tried to spell his name.

"Come on," called big Y. "Who's first?"

Big J jumped up on to the hearth; then little o; and then little e. And all the letters clapped. After that they had a lovely game of spelling. It was their favourite game. (The only one they knew, really!)

73

"Come on," called big K, "let's spell 'dog'." So little d and little o and little g got up and stood in a row and all the letters clapped again and d, o, and g bowed.

"Now, let's spell 'cat'," said big K. And c – a – t stood in a row.

"Now spell 'cake'," said big G. So little c and little a stood up again and so did little e. But, where was little k? He wasn't there! Some of the letters looked under the carpet. Big Y ran upstairs and looked in the bath-room. They searched everywhere, but they couldn't find him. Then Joe had an idea and he went out into the back yard. He looked at the place where the waste water-pipe came down from the bath-room and there he saw little k stuck in the grating.

Joe pulled him out and brushed him and took him back to the fire side. The letters *were* pleased. Then Joe said he had to go home because it was bedtime and big K said, "Would you like some cake crumbs?"

"Yes, please!" said Joe. So they gave him a bag of crumbs.

"Do come and see us again," said the letters, "any evening after the children have gone to bed."

"I will," said Joe, and he carried the cake crumbs home and gave one each to his mother and father and brothers and sisters. Then he kissed them all good night and crawled to his own little part of the crack in the wall and went to sleep.

The useful dragon

Once upon a time there lived a dragon whose name was
Komodo. He could breathe fire. And all the people who
lived near by were afraid of him. Whenever they heard him
coming they ran away and hid.

They could always hear him because Komodo had six
feet, and wore three pairs of shoes at a time and every shoe

creaked. So wherever Komodo went the people were sure to know.

One day he met a little girl who wasn't a bit afraid of him.

"Why are you so fierce?" she said. "Why do you breathe fire when you see anyone coming?"

"Well," said Komodo, "I – er – um – well – um I dunno. I never really thought about it. Shall I stop being fierce?"

"Yes, please," said the little girl, whose name was Susie.

"All right," said Komodo, "I'll try."

They said goodbye to each other, and Susie went home. By then it was beginning to get dark and Susie found that

everyone was in an awful state, because the lamplighter, whose name was Charlie, hadn't lit any of the street lamps.

He was still in bed. He stayed out so late after lighting the lamps the night before that he was still tired. So he just stayed in bed and had a lovely sleep. And ate bread and butter under the bedclothes.

The mayor, whose name was William, was furious. What was to be done about the lamps? Then Susie had an idea. She ran all the way to Komodo's cave and fetched him to the town and took him all round the streets, and he breathed fire on each lamp and lit it.

How the people cheered. They were not afraid of the dragon any more. They could see he was a friendly beast. And after that Komodo came and lit the lamps every year when Charlie went on his holiday.

Bump!

In a hole in a wall in a room in a house in a street in a town in a country in the world in the sky, there lived a mouse whose name was Albert. He lay on his bed and ate some cheese and watched a spider on the rafters trying to swing from one beam to another.

The spider was hanging by a long thread and swung as

hard as he could – once, then he swung again – twice, and again – three times, and banged his head a great big bump on the other beam, and crawled back on to his web in a very bad temper.

He sat down and thought for a bit, then came out and tried again. This time he got across.

Albert grew tired of watching the spider and got up and

went to the Zoo to see his friend the kangaroo, whose name was Bob.

Bob was wearing some new shoes, which had sponge in the soles to help him bounce better. He was practising his bouncing when Albert arrived.

"Look how high I can bounce," said Bob. And he bounced up and down.

He bounced so high he could see over the fence; then higher and he could see over the houses; then higher still,

he could see over the church steeples; then higher – and just then an aeroplane was passing and Bob bumped his head a great big bump on the underneath part of it.

"What a bump!" thought Albert. "Just like the spider's when he bumped his head on the beam."

Bob had one more bounce and he bounced as high, almost as high, as the sun. Then he went and saw his keeper, who bathed his head with warm water so that the bump didn't feel so sore. Then he had tea.

After tea, Albert went home and got some hot water and bathed the spider's bump.

"What a friend Albert is," thought the spider as he curled up on his web and went to sleep.

Please, Thank-you and Sorry

Once upon a time, Please and Thank-you were having a little talk. They were feeling very sorry for themselves. Presently they saw Sorry coming along.

"Why is it," said Sorry, "that all the other words have such a nice easy time while we have to work so hard? People are always saying, 'Please', 'Sorry' and 'Thank-you', but half the time they don't mean what they say. It isn't fair!"

"No, it *isn't* fair!" said Thank-you. "There is a lady in our street who has a little girl and she is always saying, 'Say thank-you' to her. I'm sure that when that little girl grows up she will say 'thank-you', but it won't *mean* much. And it makes me so very tired. I just don't get a moment's sleep."

"It's just as bad for me," said Please. "All day long, in every bus in the world, it's 'Fares, please! Fares, please! Fares, please!' Of course, it's nice being polite, but I am quite worn out."

Please turned to sit down and accidently trod on Thank-you's toes. "Sorry!" he said.

"There you go!" said Sorry. "Even you make me work!"

"Oh, sorry!" said Please. "I trod on Thank-you's toes so I said sorry, Sorry."

"There you go again!" said Sorry. "Will you please stop it? There, now I'm making *you* work. What shall we do to get a rest?"

They thought for a bit and then decided they would go for a nice long holiday and sleep for a whole week. Then no one in all the world would be able to say 'Please' or 'Sorry' or 'Thank-you'. And that's what they did.

When they came back from their holiday, they weren't feeling tired any more, and they didn't mind when all the people started to say 'Please' and 'Sorry' and 'Thank-you' again. It seemed *much* nicer because people had got out of the habit of mumbling 'Please' or 'Sorry' or 'Thank-you' whether they meant it or not. They only used the words when they really and truly wanted to say them, so Please, Sorry and Thank-you did not have to work quite so hard, and were not nearly so tired as they used to be.

Every year now, they go away for a holiday so that when they come back, people will remember when they say 'Please' or 'Sorry' or 'Thank-you' that the words really do mean something.

The Captain's horse

Once upon a time there was a horse who had very short legs. His name was Dick.

He was a very nice horse, but sometimes the other horses laughed at him; and once, when he was trotting along, a little worm who was crawling by, said, "Hahaha! Look at old shorty legs!"

And a little black duck swimming on the pond quacked, "Poor thing, he *has* got short legs, hasn't he!"

Dick felt very sad, "I wish I had nice long legs," he thought. "What use is a horse with short legs? Boohoohoo!" And he began to cry.

Presently he saw a soldier sitting under a tree by the roadside and he was crying too. Tears were streaming down his cheeks and making his black moustache all wet.

"Oh dear, what's the matter?" said Dick, going up to him.

"The King says I can't have any jam for tea!" said the soldier, sobbing louder than ever.

"No jam for tea!" said Dick, feeling very sorry for him. He saw that the soldier was wearing spurs on his boots and was carrying a helmet that had a big dent in it.

"No!" sobbed the soldier, whose name was Henry. "The King said that next time I dented my helmet I wouldn't have any jam for tea. Every time I ride under the archway out of the castle, I bang my head on the roof and dent my helmet. But I can't help it! My horse has got such long legs that I'm too high up. I wish I had a horse with nice short

legs like – like you!" he said, looking at Dick's short legs. "Will you be my horse?"

"Of course I will!" said Dick. And they gave each other a big hug. Henry took Dick to the castle and gave him some hay.

Next day the King ordered his buglers to blow their trumpets. So they blew, "Tarrarara tarrarara!" and all the King's soldiers got on their horses, rode out of the castle and lined up in a row, waiting for the King to come out.

When he came out he saw that everyone except Henry had a dent in his helmet and he was very angry. But first he asked Henry, "How is it you haven't got a dent in your helmet?"

"Because, Your Majesty," said Henry, "I've got a horse with nice short legs – his name's Dick."

"Why, so you have!" said the King. "Yes! Very nice short legs." Then he called out to the other soldiers, "You're very naughty to dent your helmets. You shan't have any jam for tea today. And in future, you must all ride horses with nice short legs like Dick here."

Then he told Henry he was made Captain of the Guard. And he gave Dick a new nose-bag with his name on it. He was a very happy horse.

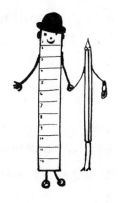

The pencil
and the ruler

Once upon a time there was a pencil which couldn't draw straight lines. It could draw curves and circles,

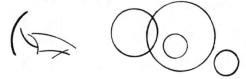

pussy-cats and little girls,

oranges and lemons and all sorts of curved things, but it

couldn't draw squares and triangles and ships, or tables and chairs.

It did want to draw straight lines more than anything else; but however hard it tried, it couldn't. It fell down and broke its point.

Then it thought, "I'll ask the cat how to draw straight lines." But the cat didn't know. She could only show him how to drink milk and purr.

Then he asked a dog. But the dog didn't know. He only wagged his tail and barked.

"What foolish animals dogs are," thought the pencil.
Then it saw, lying on the table, the most beautiful thing it had seen in its life. It was a ruler.

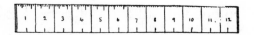

"Oh, please, will you draw some straight lines with me," the pencil said.
And the ruler replied, "I will."

They drew houses

and ships,

tables and chairs,
books and a brush and comb

and tea-pots

and Christmas trees

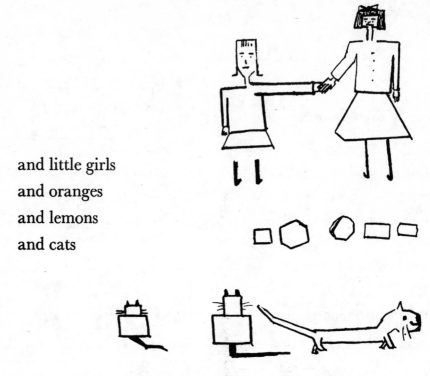

and little girls
and oranges
and lemons
and cats

and they lived happily ever after.

Hide-and-seek

Once upon a time the Dark was playing hide-and-seek with the Moon. Sometimes it hid behind houses or chimneys and kept very still while the moonlight crept round to find it.

Sometimes it would dart about, hiding behind a pussy-cat or a little dog crossing the road. It was very clever at hiding from the Moon.

But when the Sun rose, that was different.

"Just you wait!" said the Moon. "When the Sun shines, where will you hide then?"

"I'll hide behind the children going to school," said the Dark, "and be their shadows."

"That's all very well," said the Moon, "but when the children go *into* school, *then* where will you hide? Really, my dear, you had better go and hide round the other side of the world or the Sun will be sure to catch you."

"No, it won't!" said the Dark. "You wait and see!"

Well presently the Sun rose and most of the Dark went and hid round at the other side of the world and made it night there, but some little bits of Dark stayed to play with the Sun.

They had a lovely time and some pieces were people's shadows and some were pussy-cats' shadows and dogs' shadows and cows' shadows, and some were little birds' shadows and flitted across the lawn, but the Sun nearly always caught them in the end till there was only one little piece of Dark left.

"I'll catch you!" said the Sun. "No matter where you hide!"

"No you won't!" said the Dark. "I've thought of a lovely place where you'll never find me. Now don't look! And count ten while I go and hide."

So the Sun hid behind a cloud and counted ten. Then it came out to look.

"I expect it's hiding behind someone and being their shadow!" said the Sun. But though it looked everywhere, it couldn't find the Dark.

It looked all day and all the next day, but couldn't find it, and indeed it never found it at all because the Dark had found such a wonderful place to hide – in the cupboard under the stairs.

"It is nice here!" thought the Dark. "I think I'll stay here all the time." And it did.

And that's why it's always dark in the cupboard under the stairs.

The squeak

Once upon a time in the Festival Hall in London, a lady was dancing and all the people in the audience were watching and having a wonderful time. But the dancer herself was rather angry because, every time she stepped on one floorboard on the stage, it squeaked.

So after the dancing was over, she said to the manager, "There is a floorboard on this stage that squeaks every time I tread on it. How can I dance when the floorboard squeaks?"

"Oh, I'm terribly sorry!" said the manager. "I'll mend it." And after the people had gone home, and it was all dark in the theatre, the manager collected lots of nails and went out on the stage with a lighted candle. He put the candle down, and hammered the board absolutely *all* the way round so that it couldn't *possibly* squeak any more.

Next day, when the dancer came, the manager said, "Madam, my dear, I have nailed the floorboard down so that it cannot squeak any more."

"Thank-you!" said the dancer, "You *are* a nice manager."

Well, the people came in and the music played and she started to dance again, but every time she stepped on that board – it *squeaked*.

As soon as the curtain came down for the interval, she sent for the manager and she said, "I thought you said you had stopped that board squeaking! Well, listen!" And she trod on the board – and it squeaked. She trod again – and it squeaked again.

"Now," she said, "just take that board away and get one that doesn't squeak."

So the carpenter came along and the manager came with some nails and hammers and saws, and they cut the board and they picked it up and were just going to throw it away when they saw in the space underneath it, a little Teddy Bear.

"Oh, what a lovely Teddy Bear!" said the dancer, and she picked it up and gave it a hug. And as soon as she gave it a hug – it *squeaked*.

"Oh!" she said. "Now I understand! Whenever I trod on the board it made *you* squeak."

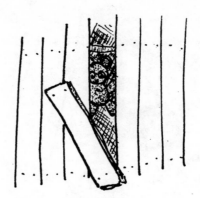

Everybody laughed. And they put the board back and the music played and the dancer danced beautifully and made all the people happy.

That night, the dancer took the Teddy Bear home. When she got there her little boy was sound asleep and she put the Teddy into his cot.

In the morning he woke up and saw it. "Look!" he said. "There's a Teddy Bear in my bed!" And he gave it a hug – and it squeaked.

Starry eagle

Once upon a time an eagle, whose name was David, lived on top of a mountain in Wales.

David liked flying high up in the air. One day he flew so high that he came to a star. There was a little house on the star. Mary and her little lamb lived there. David knocked on the door.

"I've come to tea," he said. So Mary laid the table and they all sat down.

"Would you like some toast, Eagle dear?" said Mary.

"Mm – no thank-you," said David, "I'd like to eat a little lamb."

"My! you haven't washed your claws," said Mary, and she picked David up and took him through to the kitchen to wash. While he was drying his claws she came back and whispered in the little lamb's ear.

David came back and sat down.

"Would you like some more toast, little lamb?" said Mary.

"No, thank-you," said the lamb, remembering what Mary had whispered to him. "I think I'd like some eagle."

David was surprised, and felt a bit nervous. So when Mary asked him again what he would like, he said, "I think I'd like some toast, please." So Mary gave him some. And after tea he said goodbye to Mary and her little lamb, and flew all the way home again.

Before he went to sleep that night, he looked up and saw the star shining high above him.

Ink blots

Once upon a time, a king and his beautiful daughter lived in a great palace of ice far, far away in Siberia. It was the most beautiful, sparkling palace in the world, but because it was made of ice the King was afraid it would melt one day – and then he and his daughter would have nowhere to live.

It was very cold in Siberia. Jack Frost lived there too, and the cold East Wind. They came to the King and his daughter and said, "You must tell us a story every week or we will go away, and then your palace won't be cold any more and the ice will melt and you won't have anywhere to live."

The King was in despair. "I'll never be able to think of a story every week!" he said.

But his daughter said, "Give me a pen and ink and an owl and a green umbrella, and *I* will tell them a story."

So the King gave them to her and she sat down cross-legged on a cushion and put up the green umbrella. Then she dipped the pen in the ink and gave it to the owl.

"Now," she said, "you fly up and perch on top of the umbrella and then shake the pen so that an ink blot falls down."

So the owl took the pen and perched on top of the umbrella and shook some ink down so that a big blot of ink made a funny shape on the umbrella.

The King's daughter looked at it. "Now, what does that shape look like?" she thought. "I know! It looks like a rather grumpy little dragon."

Then she told the owl to make another blot and she looked at that. Its shape was rather like a rice pudding.

"Oh do hurry up!!" said Jack Frost, impatiently. "Tell us a story!"

"All right!" said the King's daughter. "Once upon a

time there was a little dragon who wouldn't eat his rice pudding. His Granny, who was a very very old dragon, was quite upset. 'You'll never grow big and strong if you don't eat your rice pudding!' she said. 'Oh dear! What shall I do?'

"She went to the kitchen cupboard and looked in. 'Would you like some jam with it, or marmalade or honey?' she said.

"Just then her cat, Alice, came along. Alice was a big white cat with her fur singed in places because Granny sometimes breathed on her accidentally when she was giving her a cuddle.

"Alice looked up at Granny and said, 'Mieow! Baby dragons don't like jam or honey or marmalade unless it's fried.' "

"Ugh! Fancy fried marmalade!" said Jack Frost.

" 'I know what I'll do!' said Granny. She got a big baking dish and spread some rice pudding at the bottom and then a layer of red pepper and peppercorns. Then, on top, she put some more rice pudding and then a layer of black pepper and peppercorns. Then another layer of rice, then she covered it all with a great big thick layer of mustard and put it in the oven to bake.

"And that evening, the baby dragon ate *all* his rice pudding. And after that, he always ate his rice pudding and grew up to be a great big dragon who was very good at breathing fire. And that is the end of the story."

"Thank-you!" said Jack Frost.

"And a very nice story, too!" said the East Wind.

They were both very pleased and said they would come and hear a story every week and keep the ice palace cold so that it wouldn't melt.

"Thank-you, my dear!" said the King to his daughter, when they had gone. "I suppose seeing shapes in ink blots is rather like seeing pictures in the fire?"

"Yes!" said his daughter. "But we couldn't have a fire or our lovely palace would melt."

"That's true!" said the King. "You are as clever as you are beautiful!" And he gave her a kiss.

Mr Crococat

Once upon a time the Man-in-the-Moon was looking down at the world when he saw a great big dog chasing a little pussy-cat and barking as hard as he could.

"What a naughty dog!" said the Man-in-the-Moon. "I wonder who it is? It looks like Butch who lives in the High Street. Yes! It *is* Butch! I'll teach him not to do it again!"

Later that night when he was shining over Africa, he peered down looking for his friend, Mr Crococat. Mr Crococat was a very strange animal. He was a cat one end and a crocodile the other end. He was the only one in the world, and lived very quietly by himself in a little cave in Africa where no one could find him.

"Aren't you very lonely?" asked the Man-in-the-Moon.

"Oh, no!" said Mr Crococat.

"I should have thought you were," said the Man-in-the-Moon, "with no one to kiss you good night."

"Tch! Don't you understand?" said Mr Crococat. "I'm the *only* animal in the world who *always* has someone to kiss him good night. Look, I'll show you!" And he bent round in the middle and kissed himself good night.

"Good night, dear Croc!" said the cat end. "I hope you sleep well."

"Good night, Pussy, my pet!" said the crocodile end. "Pleasant dreams!"

"Hm!" said the Man-in-the-Moon. "It's got its advantages being a crococat, hasn't it?"

"Yes, it has!" said Mr Crococat. "But it's got its drawbacks too, you know."

"Oh, what's that?" asked the Man-in-the-Moon.

"Well," Mr Crococat replied, "when I walk forward the back part of me has to walk backwards. And when I walk the other way, the front part has to walk backwards. In fact, sometimes I hardly know whether I'm coming or going."

"Yes, I can see that," said the Man-in-the-Moon, "but, by the way, I wonder if you would do something for me. There's a very naughty dog called Butch who lives in

104

England and he *will* chase cats. Now, if you go there one night and let him see your cat end, he's sure to chase you, and then you can turn round and frighten him with your *crocodile* end. Then, perhaps, he won't chase cats any more."

"All right," said Mr Crococat. "I'll come."

When he got to England, the moon shone very bright in the back garden next door to Butch; and Mr Crococat lay down with his crocodile end in the shadow of a tree, but his cat end was in the moonlight.

When Butch saw what he thought was a pussy-cat, he barked and jumped over the fence to chase him. But when he got there it wasn't a pussy-cat: it was a *crocodile* – looking very fierce.

Poor Butch turned and ran and didn't stop till he was safe in his basket in the kitchen.

"Whew! I'll never chase cats again!" he thought.

How the Man-in-the-Moon and Mr Crococat laughed!

A little later Mr Crococat yawned. "I think I'll have a little sleep now," he said and lay down.

"Good night, dear Croc," said the cat end.

"Good night, Pussy, my pet," said the crocodile end. "Pleasant dreams."

The beetle and
the bulldozer

Once upon a time, a tiger whose name was Sam lay sound asleep in bed. The sun shone down, it was a very hot day, but still Sam slept. He was a very lazy tiger, and sometimes slept nearly all day.

Just then a beetle walked by.

 "My! My", said the beetle, whose name was William. "That bed looks comfortable." And he climbed into bed beside Sam. Soon he was fast asleep.

When Sam woke up he was surprised to see William. He didn't really like a beetle in his bed at all. So he took a deep breath, and blew as hard as he could. William woke up.

"What a windy day it is," he said to himself, as he clung to the sheets." Sam blew as hard as he could, but he couldn't blow William out of bed.

So then he thought, "If I give him a big wet lick on his face, perhaps he'll think it is raining, and get up and hurry home." So he gave him a big lick.

"Hm!" Seems to be a very wet day," said William, and he crawled under the bed-clothes, but he didn't get up.

Poor Sam! What was he to do to make William go away? He got up and went through the forest to the house where there was a bulldozer. The bulldozer's name was Butch.

"Will you please help me push a beetle out of my bed?" said Sam.

"Yes, I will," said Butch, and he went to where Sam's bed was and he started to push William out of bed.

William hung on as hard as he could. Butch pushed and pushed and all the animals in the forest came to watch.

What a struggle it was. Butch pushed. And William pushed.
Backwards and forwards they went.

At last William was pushed right out of bed. And he went
home to tell his brothers and sisters about his great fight
with Butch the Bulldozer.

Now Butch was so tired after the fight, and he looked at
Sam's nice, comfortable bed, and he thought, "I'll just lie
down and have a little sleep."

Sam was annoyed. It was bad enough to have a beetle in
his bed, but a bulldozer was worse.

So he went and got some water and some oil, and he put
them down some way away from the bed. Then he woke
Butch up.

"Are you hungry, Butch?" he said.

"Yes," said Butch.

"There's some nice oil and water over there," said Sam, and he pointed to the place where he had left the oil and water. Butch was pleased. He jumped out of bed and ran over to the oil and water.

Immediately he was gone, Sam jumped into the bed. "Now I've got the bed all to myself," he said, "I'm going to have a lovely sleep."

So he ate some bread and butter and had a drink of milk and then went to sleep.

The station who
wouldn't keep still

Once upon a time there was a king whose name was Samuel. He was sitting on his throne one afternoon thinking how nice it would be to go for a ride on a railway train to see his Granny. So he said goodbye to the Queen and set off.

When he got to Waterloo Station, he was just going to step off the escalator on to the platform when he heard the station say, "I would like a cup of tea," and when King Samuel stepped out . . . the station wasn't there.

He *was* surprised. He was standing on nothing!

"Oh, what a nuisance," said the King. "I'll miss the train and Granny will be furious.

"Come back at once!" he called.

But the station wouldn't. "No! Not till I've finished my tea," it said.

When it had finished tea, the station came back and King Samuel caught the train. Off they went. *Chuff, chuff, chuff!*

After they had gone a little way, they saw a cow in a field by the railway line. So the train stopped.

"Are we going the right way to Granny's house?" asked the engine-driver.

"Oh, yes!" said the cow. "Can I come too?"

"Yes, you can," said the engine-driver. "Jump in!"

So Sally, that was the cow's name, jumped in and away they went again. They had hardly gone a few yards when they heard a great panting and blowing behind them. They looked round and there just behind them, hurrying as fast as it could, was Waterloo Station.

"Can I come too?" it said.

"Of course!" said King Samuel. So they all went together and soon arrived at Granny's house.

She was surprised to see such a crowd. There was the engine-driver and Sally and King Samuel and, last of all, Waterloo Station itself.

Granny was pleased to see them and gave them all a cup of tea and, after tea, King Samuel said, "It's time to go home. I've got to be at Waterloo Station at five o'clock."

"Then, there's no need to hurry," said Granny, "because Waterloo Station is right here."

"Now that's true!" said the King. "That will save a lot of travelling. In that case we've all time for another cup of tea."

So Granny made some more tea, and after tea they all played until five o'clock. Then they said goodbye to Granny and got to Waterloo Station – and there they were, where they had started from! Except for Sally, the cow, who caught a slow train home.

"What a nice station you are," thought the King, as he said goodbye. "I must go now. The Queen will be expecting me. Do visit us sometime, won't you?"

Snow

Once upon a time, long, long, ago, there lived a little girl who had never seen the snow. Her name was Lin, and she lived in China.

One day, when Lin was walking in the garden with her pussy-cat whose name was Cheng Pu, she felt sad.

"I feel sad, Cheng Pu," she said.

"Mieow!" said Cheng Pu, as if he understood.

"You know, I've never seen the snow, and I *would* so like to."

"Mieow!" said Cheng Pu again.

That evening, in the garden after Lin had gone to bed and no one was near, the flowers began to talk to each other.

"Fancy," said a tall yellow hollyhock to a little blue pansy, "Lin has never seen the snow. She is so kind and waters us every day. I wish we could help her."

"I know what to do," said the South Wind, who was blowing there. It blew far, far away to the North across deserts and mountains and green valleys until, at last, it came to the North Pole where the North Wind lived.

"What are you doing here?" shouted the North Wind when it saw the South Wind. "Go away, or I'll chase you!"

"Ha, ha, ha!" laughed the South Wind. "You can't catch me!"

"Oh, can't I" roared the North Wind. "We'll soon see about that." And it chased after the South Wind.

But the South Wind turned round and blew all the way back to China, and the North Wind followed as fast as it could. But it couldn't catch the South Wind. It *was* cold though, and the clouds all shivered when the North Wind came by, and they stopped raining – and snowed.

When the North Wind found it couldn't catch the South Wind, it went back to the North Pole in a horrid temper, and blew so hard that even the polar bears shivered.

Next morning when Lin came into the garden, she saw it was covered with snow.

"How softly white and beautiful everything is!" she said. "Come and look, Cheng Pu. It must be snow!"

"Mieow!" said Cheng Pu.

Soon the South Wind blew and melted the snow, and the sun came out and warmed the flowers. Lin was very happy.

The policeman's horse

Once upon a time there was a very naughty police horse whose name was Harry, and a rather naughty policeman, too, whose name was Arthur.

Arthur, dressed in his blue uniform with his truncheon by his side, used to ride through London mounted on Harry the horse.

Harry liked following the buses that crawled slowly along in the traffic and breathing on the back window till it was all misty. Then Arthur leant forward in the saddle and, with his finger, he would draw faces on the misty window, which made Harry laugh.

But they were so busy, Harry following the buses and breathing on the window, and Arthur drawing faces, that they never had time to catch any burglars. So the inspector at the police station, whose name was Reginald, said to the police sergeant one morning, "Sergeant!"

"Yes, sir!" said the sergeant, standing to attention and saluting.

"Sergeant," said Reginald, "why doesn't Arthur catch any burglars?"

"I don't know, sir," said the sergeant.

"Well, find out, Sergeant, there's a good chap," said Inspector Reginald.

"Yes, sir!" said George (that was the sergeant's name), and saluted again. Then he went out and got on his horse, which was a very good horse and never breathed on the back of buses, and rode down the street to see if he could find Harry and Arthur and see what they were up to.

Then he saw them. There was Harry breathing on the back window of a bus to make it misty and Arthur leaning forward and drawing a picture on it.

"Oh, they *are* naughty!" said Sergeant George. "Still, it would be rather fun, wouldn't it?" So he edged his horse up behind a bus so that it breathed on the back window. Then he leant forward and drew a picture of Inspector Reginald on the glass with his finger. And another police-man saw him and thought it would be fun, too. After that, all the policeman's horses started to follow buses and breathe on the windows so that the policemen riding them could draw pictures.

And all the burglars were very surprised because the policemen were so busy drawing that they never came to arrest them any more.

"I wonder what has happened to the policemen?" they said, and they went and looked and saw that they were drawing on the windows on the backs of the buses.

"What fun!" said the burglars, and they all went and stopped being burglars and bought horses instead so that they could breathe on the bus windows for them to draw pictures too.

The head policeman of all London was very pleased about that, so he sent for Harry and Arthur.

"You are both very clever!" he said, and made Arthur a sergeant.

The Moon's overcoat

Once upon a time, on a cold winter's night, the Moon was looking down at the world. Everyone was wearing a warm overcoat.

"I would like one, too," it thought. So it said to the Man-in-the-Moon, "Will you make me a warm overcoat, please?"

"All right!" said the Man-in-the-Moon. So he got out his sewing machine and some cloth and some thread and some buttons and his scissors and tape measure.

First of all he measured the Moon, then he cut the cloth and sewed it up. Then he put on the buttons. Within a fortnight the coat was ready, and he said, "Now, come and try it on."

The Moon tried it on, but it was much too big.

"That's funny!" said the Man-in-the-Moon, scratching his head. He got out his tape measure and measured the Moon again. It was much smaller this time. So he got his scissors and sewing machine and thread and made the coat smaller.

A fortnight later, when he'd done the alteration, the Moon tried it on once more. This time it was much

too small because somehow the Moon had grown fatter.

"How can I make you an overcoat that fits if you keep getting fat and thin like that?" said the Man-in-the-Moon. He was quite angry, but being a kind man he said, "I'll make you two overcoats. One for when you are fat and one for when you are thin."

"Thank-you!" said the Moon.

When the coats were made it tried them on and they fitted very well. But of course, when it had an overcoat on, it couldn't shine properly.

When the people in the world looked up they could see the stars shining, but they couldn't see the Moon, and they felt sad.

"That will never do!" said the Man-in-the-Moon. "You must shine sometimes so that the children going to bed can see you."

"All right!" said the Moon and took off its overcoat and shone.

The people down in the world looked up and saw it and were very pleased, especially the children. Sometimes they saw the Moon was fat and sometimes it was a thin crescent moon, and sometimes they couldn't see it at all.

"Ah!" they said. "It's got its overcoat on."

"Yes," said the Moon. "I have!" And it's lovely and warm."

But it didn't keep it on for long and soon shone again, high up in the sky away above the clouds. When the little stars heard about the Moon's overcoat they were very interested.

"Let's go and ask the Man-in-the-Moon to make us overcoats," they said.

"Oh no!" said the Man-in-the-Moon. "I couldn't possibly make an overcoat for every star in the sky. It would take me years and years and *years*. Besides, I haven't enough material."

Then he had an idea and he called to all the little clouds. He told the clouds to go and wrap themselves round the stars at night and keep them warm.

The stars were thrilled. But when the Moon took off its overcoat and started shining by itself, it grew lonely. So whenever the Moon took off its overcoat, the stars would give the clouds a night off. And then they winked and twinkled their hardest at the Moon. The Moon was very pleased. And so were all the people down in the world below, especially the children.

The thoughtful beetle

Uncle Fred lived at No. 8 Westwind Road, Whitechapel. On one side of his picture in the front room there stood a rose in a little glass jar, and on the other, a clock whose name was Tyma.

"What a useless thing a clock is," said the rose to itself, "it doesn't smell at all. Only things that smell nice are really beautiful."

"What a foolish thing a rose is," thought the clock, "it

doesn't show the time, and only things that tell the time
are really beautiful."

Just then a black beetle walked by, and he looked at the
rose and the clock.

"Hmmm! they are not very black, are they?" he thought.
"Poor things!" and he walked on. He was going to see his
grandmother it was her birthday.

Then a sparrow looked in at the window and saw the
clock and the rose. "Huh! what's the good of ticking and
smelling if you can't fly? What is more beautiful than
flying?"

"Swimming," said a goldfish, who was in a bowl of
water at the other side of the room.

"Mieowing," said a cat, jumping from the window-sill
into the garden.

"Eating," said a pig who lived in a sty in the garden next door.

"Making the trees wave," said the wind, as it rushed down the garden path.

"Making the wind blow," said the trees, as they waved at the bottom of the garden.

The rose and the clock were still arguing when Uncle Fred came in with his wife.

"And what are you good for?" they said to him.

"Well," said Uncle Fred, "it all depends on how you look at it I suppose."

"Of course it does," said his wife. "I think you are nice to kiss," and she kissed him.